It was Friday night, and Mom and Dad were headed to the movies. "The babysitter will be here any moment now," they said.

"I think she may have arrived," said my big sister. It was . . .

THE BABYSITTER FROM ANOTHER PLANET

STEPHEN SAVAGE

NEAL PORTER BOOKS

HOLIDAY HOUSE / NEW YORK

She took some getting used to . . .

but she knew just what to do.

She helped us with our homework.

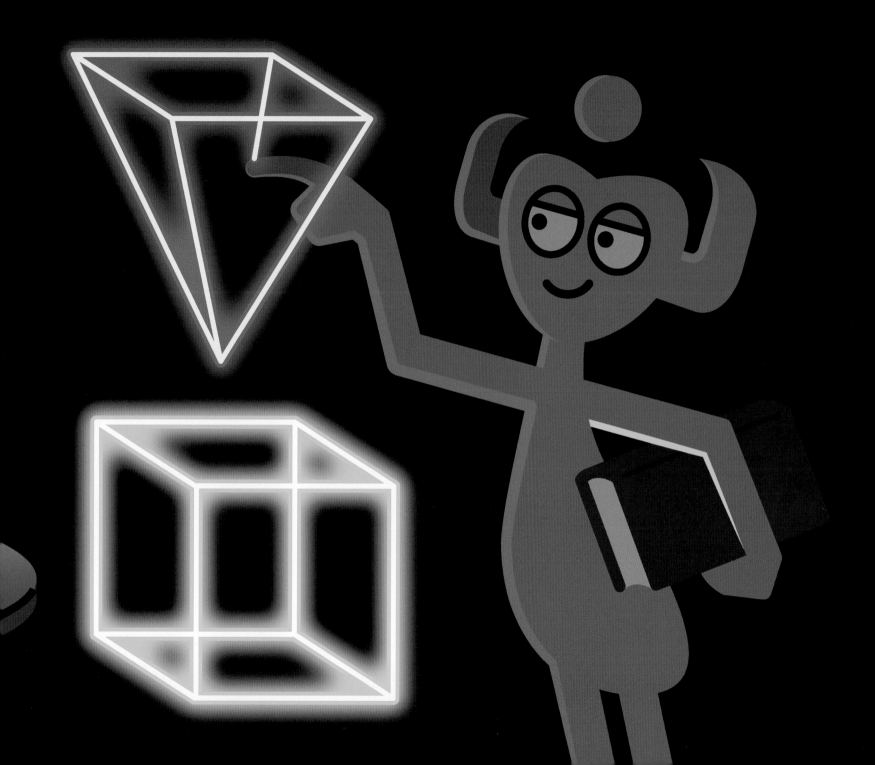

And made sure we brushed our teeth.

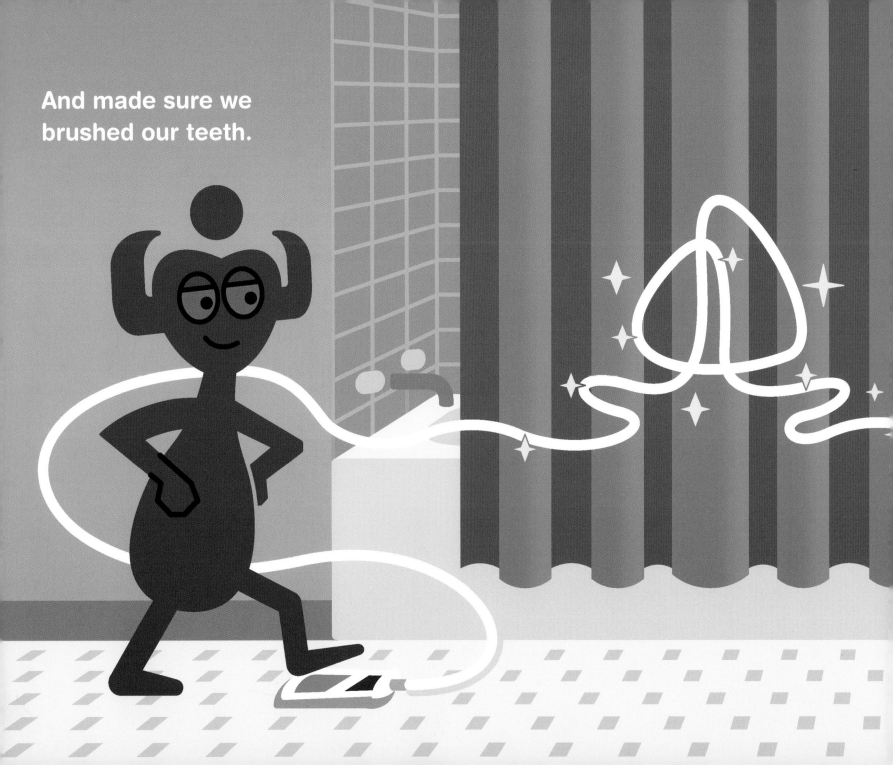

She read us
a bedtime story.

And sang us her
favorite lullaby.

But we weren't tired!

We didn't even notice Mom and Dad
pulling into the driveway.

"Quick! Jump into bed!" I said.

"Oh no!
The night-light's
not working."

The Babysitter from Another Planet
just smiled.

The next Friday, Mom and Dad went to the movies again. This time our babysitter was just a plain old human.

So we called the Babysitter from Another Planet.

And this time . . .

she brought friends.

For Brenda Bowen

Neal Porter Books

Text and illustrations copyright © 2019 by Stephen Savage
All Rights Reserved
HOLIDAY HOUSE is registered in the U.S. Patent and Trademark Office.
Printed and Bound in July 2018 at Tien Wah Press, Johor Bahru, Johor, Malaysia.
The artwork was created using digital techniques.
www.holidayhouse.com
First Edition
1   3   5   7   9   10   8   6   4   2

Library of Congress Cataloging-in-Publication Data

Names: Savage, Stephen, 1965- author, illustrator.
Title: The babysitter from another planet / by Stephen Savage.
Description: First edition. | New York : Holiday House, [2019] | "Neal Porter
Books." | Summary: "The kids are in for a treat when their parents leave
them with an extraterrestrial babysitter"— Provided by publisher.
Identifiers: LCCN 2018011511 | ISBN 9780823441471 (hardcover)
Subjects: | CYAC: Babysitters—Fiction. | Extraterrestrial beings—Fiction.
Classification: LCC PZ7.S2615 Bab 2019 | DDC [E] —dc23 LC record available at https://lccn.loc.gov/2018011511